'Who could that be?' she wondered.

**Dear Witch,**

Please join me for a picnic. I will be waiting at the swamp from one o'clock.

**Love, Troll**

Pretty

CANIZALES

Early one morning, the witch was making
a nice cup of tea when a message arrived.

PING!

"A picnic?" said the witch.
"How nice! I'd better get ready."

Now she just had to pick
the perfect outfit for her date.

But there were so many options . . .

Finally the witch made her choice
and set off for the swamp.

The witch hadn't gone far
when she met a squirrel.

"Hello Squirrel,"
she said. "Guess what?
I'm on my way to a date!"

"What?" said the squirrel.
"You can't go like that.
Look at your back — it's so crooked!
Can't you fix it with your wand?
Then you'd look pretty."

'Why not?' thought the witch.

So she waved her wand,
and just like that she had
a nice straight back.

Further along the path the witch bumped into a rabbit.

"Hello Rabbit," she said. "I'm off to meet the troll for a picnic!"

"Are you sure that's a good idea?" said the rabbit, twitching his whiskers. "Have you seen your nose lately? It's horribly lumpy! Change it with your wand and then you'll be **pretty**."

'It can't hurt,' thought the witch.

So she waved her wand, and just like that she had a nice straight back *and* a neat little nose.

The witch kept walking when a fox appeared from behind a tree.

**"Hello Fox,"** she said.
"I can't stop to talk, I'm going on a date with the troll."

"Well I wouldn't go like that,"
said the fox. "What about that big pointy chin of yours?
If you lose that, you might look quite **pretty**."

'I may as well,' thought the witch.

So she waved her wand,
and just like that she had
a nice straight back,
a neat little nose *and*
a very dainty chin.

The witch had nearly reached the
swamp when she saw a mouse.

"Hello Mouse," she said
with a sigh. "I'm in a bit of a hurry . . .
I'll be late to meet the troll."

The mouse squeaked, "Eek, but look at your hair!
It's so wiry and tangled — can't you do something about it? You'd look so **pretty**."

The witch rolled her eyes. This was getting silly.

But she waved her wand anyway,
and just like that she had
a nice straight back,
a neat little nose,
a very dainty chin *and*
sleek, wavy hair.

'Now I must look **pretty**,'
she thought.

At long last, the witch arrived at the swamp.

"Hello Troll," she said.
"I'm starving!"

"Who are you?" grumbled the troll. "I'm waiting for the witch. She'll be here any moment. Go away!"

"But . . . I *am* the witch," said the witch. "Can't you tell?

I just made myself look pretty for our date."

"You don't fool me," replied the troll. "The witch I invited has a crooked back, a lumpy nose, a big pointy chin and wiry hair — you look nothing like her."

The witch pulled out a
mirror and gasped. A very
different witch was looking
back at her . . .

"Argh!" she screamed.
"That's not me!"

"**What a let-down,**" muttered the troll.
He scooped up the picnic and stomped away.

The witch pulled out her wand and ZAP!

Just like that she had
a crooked back,
a lumpy nose,
a big pointy chin *and*
wiry hair.

'That's better,' she thought.

She never should have listened to those animals — they had completely ruined her date. If only there was a way to get her own back *and* have the perfect picnic . . .

"Hmmm . . ."

The next day, the witch called the troll and invited him on a date. She picked the perfect outfit, packed up a fresh picnic and set off for the swamp.

"What do you think of the food?" she asked.

"It's delicious," said the troll.
"What did you put in it?"

The witch smiled to herself.

"Oh, just a few things I picked up on my way . . ."

## Starter

*Spicy squirrel soup sprinkled with*
*mouldy cheese shavings —*
*a dish best served cold*

## Main

*'Vegetable patch' stew —*
*slow-cooked cauldron of rabbit in*
*a squashed-slug sauce, served with*
*maggoty carrots and witch-nose*
*potatoes*

# Picnic MENU

## Sides
Foxy french fries drizzled
with a sticky fly and
frogspawn sauce

## Dessert
Furry mouse mousse
scattered with super-sticky
chocolate droppings